The Great Big Enormous Turnip

Retold by Michèle Dufresne
Illustrated by Michelle Morse

PIONEER VALLEY EDUCATIONAL PRESS, INC.

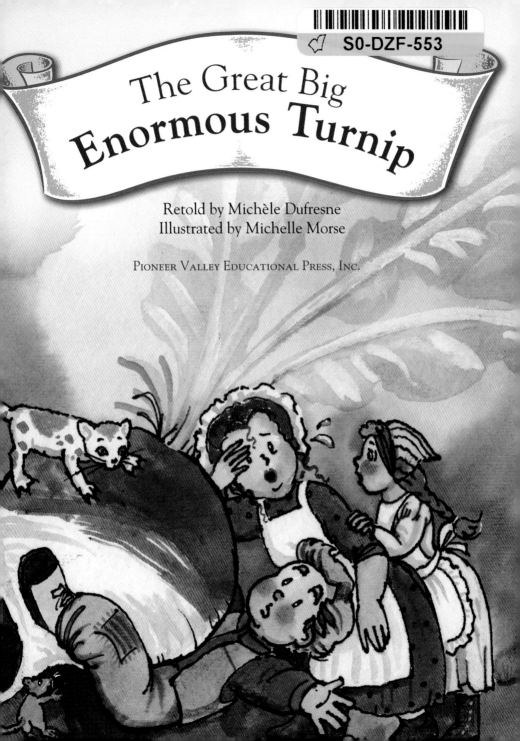

Once upon a time,
a farmer planted
a little turnip seed.

The farmer said,
"Grow, little turnip seed."
And the turnip grew
and grew and GREW!

It grew to be a great big,
enormous turnip!

Then one day, the farmer
went to pull up the turnip.
He pulled and he pulled.
He pulled and he pulled again,
but the turnip did not
come out.

The farmer called
to his wife,
"Come and help me pull out
this great big, enormous turnip."

So the farmer's wife
pulled the farmer.
The farmer pulled
the turnip.
They pulled and pulled,
but the turnip
did not come out.

The farmer's wife
called to the daughter,
"Come and help us pull out
this great big, enormous turnip."

So the daughter pulled
the farmer's wife.
The farmer's wife
pulled the farmer.

The farmer pulled the turnip.
They pulled and pulled,
but the turnip
did not come out.

The daughter called
to the cat,
"Come and help us pull out
this great big, enormous turnip."

So the cat pulled the daughter
and the daughter pulled
the farmer's wife.

The farmer's wife pulled
the farmer.
The farmer pulled the turnip.
They pulled and pulled,
but STILL the turnip
did not come out.

The cat called
to the mouse,
"Come and help us pull out
this great big, enormous turnip."

So the mouse pulled the cat.
The cat pulled the daughter.

The daughter pulled
the farmer's wife.
The farmer's wife
pulled the farmer.
The farmer pulled the turnip.
They pulled and pulled
and pulled ...

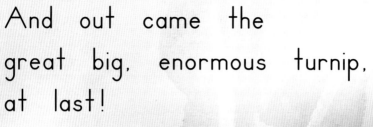

And out came the
great big, enormous turnip,
at last!